AF306764

The Royal Picture Alphabet

John Leighton

Imprint

This book is part of TREDITION CLASSICS

Author: John Leighton
Cover design: Buchgut, Berlin – Germany

Publisher: tredition GmbH, Hamburg - Germany
ISBN: 978-3-8472-3868-3

www.tredition.com
www.tredition.de

[Pg 1]

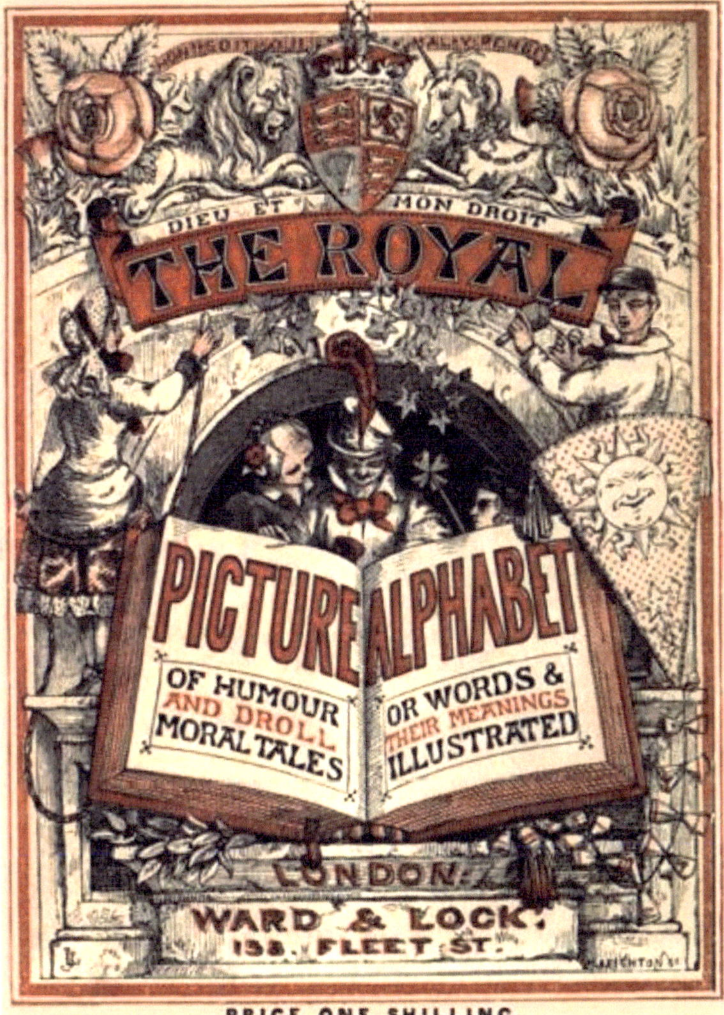

DIEU ET MON DROIT
THE ROYAL
PICTURE ALPHABET
OF HUMOUR
AND DROLL
MORAL TALES
OR WORDS &
THEIR MEANINGS
ILLUSTRATED
LONDON:
WARD & LOCK,
158, FLEET ST.
PRICE ONE SHILLING.

[Pg 2]

LAUGH AND LEARN

THE
ROYAL
PICTURE ALPHABET.

LONDON:

WARD AND LOCK,

158, FLEET STREET.

 POETICAL PREFACE

TO THE

ROYAL PIC-TURE ALPHA-BET.

TO PRECEPTORS.

With learning may laughter be found,
"'Tis good to be merry and wise;"
To gaily get over the ground,
As higher and higher we rise.

Some children their letters may learn,
While others will surely do more,
As the subjects suggestively turn
To matters not thought of before.

Descriptions and pictures combined
Are here made attractive and clear;
So suited that children may find
From error the truth to appear.

Aa. Ablution,
The Act of Cleansing.

The little sweep has washed his face,
But not as we advise:
For black as soot he's made the soap,
And rubbed it in his eyes.

[Pg 7]

Bb.   Barter,
               Exchange.

Here's Master Mack presenting fruit,
Of which he makes display;
He knows he'll soon have Lucy's rope,
And with it skip away.

[Pg 8]

Cc.   Catastrophe, *a Final Event*
        (*generally unhappy*).

"Oh here's a sad catastrophe!"
Was Mrs. Blossom's cry —
Then — "Water! water! bring to me —
Or all my fish will die."

[Pg 9]

Dd.   DELIGHTFUL,
       Pleasant, Charming.

These boys are bathing in the stream
When they should be at school:
The master's coming round to see
Who disregards his rule.

[Pg 10]

Ee.   Eccentricity,
       Irregularity, Strangeness.

We often see things seeming strange;
But scarce so strange as this: —
Here everything is mis-applied,
Here every change amiss.

[Pg 11]

14

Ff.   Fraud,
Deceit, Trick, Artifice, Cheat.

Here is Pat Murphy, fast asleep.
And there is Neddy Bray:
The thief a watchful eye doth keep
Until he gets away.

[Pg 12]

Genius,
Mental Power, Faculty.

A little boy with little slate
May sometimes make more clear
The little thoughts that he would state
Than can by words appear.

[Pg 13]

Hh. Horror,
Terror, Dread.

This little harmless speckled frog
Seems Lady Townsend's dread:
I fear she'll run away and cry,
And hide her silly head.

[Pg 14]

ICHABOD AT THE JAM.

Ii. Jj. Ichabod, *a Christian Name.*
Jam, *a Conserve of Fruits.*

Enough is good, excess is bad:
Yet Ichabod you see,
Will with the jam his stomach cram,
Until they disagree.

[Pg 15]

Kk.   Knowing,
Conscious, Intelligent.

Tho' horses know both beans and corn,
And snuff them in the wind;
They also all know Jemmy Small,
And what he holds behind.

[Pg 16]

Ll.   Lucky,
Fortunate, Happy by Chance.

We must admire, in Lovebook's case.
The prompt decision made:
As he could not have gained the wood
If time had been delayed.

[Pg 17]

Mm.   Mimic,
        Imitative, Burlesque.

The Gentleman, who struts so fine,
Unconscious seems to be
Of Imitation by the boy
Who has the street-door key.

[Pg 18]

Nn.   Negligence,
  Heedlessness, Carelessness.

The character Tom Slowboy bears
Would much against him tell—
For any work that's wanted done,
Or even play done well.

[Pg 19]

Oo.　　　Obstinacy,
　　　Stubbornness, Waywardness.

The obstinacy of the pig
Is nature—as you see:
But boys and girls who have a mind
Should never stubborn be.

[Pg 20]

Pp.   Pets,
Favourites, Spoilt Fondlings.

Some people say that Aunty Gray
To animals is kind;
We think, instead, they are over fed,
And kept too much confined.

[Pg 21]

Qq.   Quandary,
A Doubt, a Difficulty.

Dame Partlet's in difficulty
And looks around with doubt:
Let's hope, as she some way got in,
She may some way get out.

[Pg 22]

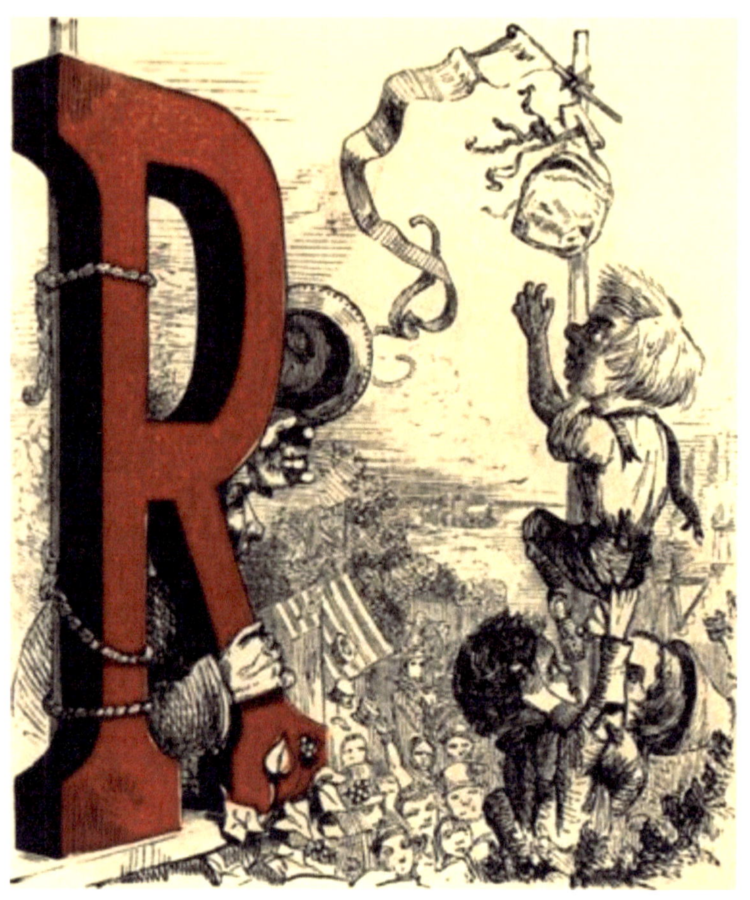

Rr.   Rivalry,
Competition, Emulation.

In every competition prize
This should be kept in view —
Whoever wins should be the one
Who does deserve it, too.

[Pg 23]

Ss.   Sluggard,
      An Inactive, Lazy Fellow.

To lie so many hours in bed
You surely must be ill—
And need some physic, Master Ned,
As birch, or draught, or pill!

[Pg 24]

Tt. Topsy-Turvy,
Upside Down, Bottom Top.

Here's Topsy-Turvy, upside down,
The ceiling seems the base:
Reverse the ground and 'twill be found
The things are out of place.

[Pg 25]

UNCOMMON VEGETATION.

Uu.Vv.   Uncommon, *Rare, not Frequent.*
          Vegetation, *the Power of Growth.*

Th' uncommon vegetation, here,
With art has much to do:
The trees are nature, but the fruit
Uncommon and untrue.

[Pg 26]

Ww.   Wonder,
            Admiration, Astonishment.

The wise may live and wonder still,
However much they know,
But simple Giles has wonder found
Within the penny show.

[Pg 27]

no english word begins with this letter .

Xx.   Xantippe,
       A Greek Matron, Wife of Socrates.

Here's Socrates and Xantippe—
Philosopher and wife—
For gentleness renowned was he;
She, better known for strife.

[Pg 28]

Yy. Yearn,
To Grieve, to Vex.

Miss Cross has tried to reach the grapes,
She's tried and tried again—
And now she's vexed to think that all
Her efforts are in vain.

[Pg 29]

Zz. Zany,
A Buffoon, a Merry Andrew.

Here's Zany reading in a book —
With heels above his head —
And, judging by his laughing look,
Finds fun in what he's read.

ABLUTION.—Poor little fellow, you are certainly making comical faces: I fear the soap has got into your eyes, and that you will make that towel very black indeed. All boys, when they wash themselves, should take care to rinse off the soap and dirt before using the towel. To make the poor little sweep quite clean would take much washing. I should like to see the soap and water a little cleaner. Many of us have nice wash-stands and baths of marble, but this poor little fellow must make the best of what he can get. See how cleverly he has put a brick under the broken leg of the stool to prop it. I like to see boys clever and ingenious.

BARTER.—Miss Lucy Hart was a nice girl, but rather thoughtless, little regarding any time but the present—new things in her eyes being the prettiest and the best;—thus, she would cast away old toys for new ones, as if she were not likely to want them again. See, Master George McGregor is bartering for her skipping-rope; offering some fruit in exchange for it. The fruit he has picked off the tree without permission. I know Lucy's mamma will be vexed; for not only will the fruit soon be gone, and the skip-rope wanted again, but it was a present from Papa. The plaything cost far more than a little fruit, which will be quickly eaten, and possibly make Lucy unwell after so much as she has had to-day.

CATASTROPHE.—Poor dear lady! has the cat tried to help himself to a gold fish, and overturned the handsome glass vase? Naughty Tom! greedy puss! I am sure kind Mrs. Blossom always feeds you well; and I think you know that you have done wrong, or you would not run so fast over the rails into Admiral Seaworth's garden, where he keeps his large dog Neptune, who may bark and send you back in a fright.

Poor fish, see how they gasp!—run and fetch some water, or they will die. Men drown in water, but fish cannot live out of it. It is the nature of cats to catch mice and birds—so that we should keep our little favourites out of their reach.

DELIGHTFUL.—These boys, I fear, are bathing without their parents' consent, which is very wrong, indeed. It is very pleasant in the water on a fine day; but little boys should not go there, as it might be deep, and they might become cramped in their limbs, and be drowned when no one was near, as many naughty boys have been before now.

It is proper that boys should learn to swim, when with Papa or some kind friend, but not as these boys have. I feel just sure they have played the truant—as I see the village school-master, with his little dog, coming over the rustic bridge to catch them.

I think that the letter D might, in this case, stand for Disobedient as well as Delightful.

ECCENTRICITY.—What have we here?—a very odd, comical picture, indeed! What a strange fellow, to put his hat upon the fire, and a saucepan on his head. I do declare he has his trowsers and waistcoat on wrong side before. See, he has taken the poker for a walking-stick, put a greasy candle in the book, and the eggs upon the floor. Why a small baby-boy would not do this: the poor fellow must be out of his right mind. You may laugh at this odd picture for it is very ridiculous, and will hurt no one; but good children should never make sport of those who are deformed in mind or body, for it is not a fault but a misfortune to be so.

FRAUD.—Patrick Murphy—commonly called, for shortness, Pat—was a very stupid little man; he reared pigs, and had he been sober, would have by this time saved a little property; but, no, Pat liked beer and strong drink: so that upon market-days he was far less sensible than his own jackass—which did know its way home—and for a long time took back foolish tipsy Pat safely; until one day, the roads being very bad, the cart came to a stop, and Neddy could pull no further. A rogue passing, seeing Pat asleep, unloosed the donkey from the cart, leaving Pat to awake, and much wonder what could have become of Neddy Bray, the donkey.

It was very wrong of the man to take Pat's donkey, although Pat was a drunken fellow.

[Pg 31] GENIUS.—Bravo! my little Artist. I dare say if you try again you will improve upon your first attempt. All people should learn to draw, that they may be able to describe a form in a very few lines, making things intelligible at sight which could not be described in any other way. A little knowledge of drawing will lead to a love of pictures and delight in the beautiful works of nature. Giotto, a great painter, who lived many hundred years ago, was but a poor shepherd-boy, who amused himself by drawing portraits of his sheep as he tended them on the hills; from rude attempts he rose to be a great artist, whose works are treasured by kings and princes. I dare say you may some day see some of the works of Giotto, the great Italian painter.

HORROR.—This drawing represents little Lady Selina Jemima Townsend as she appeared when afraid. Afraid—of what? Why, a poor tiny reptile, a harmless frog, that had jumped into her hat full of daisies, with a croak, as much as to say—"How do you do? Good morning, Lady Townsend; I am glad to see you down in the country." But what do you think she did? Why, the little lady scampered away as fast as she could to her governess, in whose dress she hid her face, crying,—saying she had seen "a nasty horrid thing." For this her governess reproved her, saying, "God created nothing in vain." Frogs are harmless and beautiful when in the water, through which they can swim and dive with wonderful ease.

ICHABOD AT THE JAM.—Ichabod is an odd name, but such is the name of the little boy in the picture. He was much pampered by his parents, and never knew when he had had enough. Ichabod would cry for things to eat, then cry again because he could eat no more, and after all cry, because eating made him feel sick and ill: but that was not all; Ichabod was, I am ashamed to say, a thief. He stole the jam when his mother thought he was asleep in bed. See, Betty the maid has heard a noise, and caught the rogue in the act. To-morrow and for many days Ichabod will be ill in bed, and have to take much nasty physic. I wish he had *mis*-taken the mustard for honey, and burnt his naughty, fibbing tongue.

KNOWING.—Ah! ah! Jemmy Small. I fear the steeds are too knowing for you to-day. They appear conscious: they would like the beans and corn you have in the sieve, but do not like the halter you are hiding behind your back. More than one has kicked up his heels, as much as to say—"Catch me if you can!" You seem to think, as you bite the straw in your mouth, that they may give you a pretty run. I know Bob, the pony, will not be soon caught.

Horses and other animals like play much better than work, but good boys and girls ought to love both, and not require sweetmeats to induce them to do their duty—for they have intellects of a high order, and may become clever men and women.

LUCKY.—Master Lovebook was indeed lucky in his escape from the Bull—and I will tell you how it happened: In going to school, this young gentleman had to go round by the wood and across the meadows, when one day he observed a savage bull making towards him; alarmed, he did not run crying anywhere, but considered one moment, and made back the shortest way to the wood, with all speed for the posts, just as the savage animal was going to toss him high in the air.

Master Lovebook was unfortunate in meeting the bull, but fortunate in having the posts between him and the infuriated animal.

In danger, brave little boys never cry, but think what is the best to be done.

MIMIC.—To be vain of anything is not right, and to be proud of fine clothes very silly indeed. The young gentleman in the picture, I think, is vain. See, he is smoking a cigar, and if we may judge by the expression of his face, we may presume that he does not fully enjoy it. As he struts along the rude boys ridicule him. See the boy behind mimicking his airs and graces—using the handle of the door-key for an eye-glass. I fear that lad's mirth will soon be changed into sorrow—for the jug must be broken against the post, and the beer spilled—so that in turn he will be laughed at.

We cannot help smiling at the little coxcomb, although at the same time we pity him.

[Pg 32] NEGLIGENCE.—Here is Tommy Slowboy, the lowest boy in the day-school, too idle to learn or even play. See how vacantly he stands gaping at the men clearing the snow from the house-tops, with his hand in his pocket because he has lost his glove, having placed the hot shoulder of mutton down in the cold snow. No wonder the first dog passing helps itself to the joint. Tom will not only be chid, but have to go without his dinner. Yet, what cares Tom for scolding or anything else, he who is so neglectful of duty?

Mind that you strive to learn early, that you may become wise and happy hereafter. Look at the picture of Tommy Slowboy, and avoid apathy and indolence.

OBSTINACY.—Obstinacy is a sad thing. See the naughty Pig in the picture, how he pulls in the opposite direction. Master Pig will be obliged to go into the sty, and very likely get the whip for his pains; like a wayward child that gets chid for disobedience. I hope there are very few disobedient young ladies and gentlemen, like the perverse pig. The pig is a stupid animal: but I have heard of a learned pig that could tell his letters, pointing to them with his snout; but most swine are dirty in their ways, and not at all particular—little caring so long as they can eat, grunt, and sleep. The pig will often lie in the dirtiest corner of his house, and stand in its trough of food.

PETS.—Here is a portrait of Aunt Gray feeding her Pets, or rather stuffing the poor monkey. Some people say Miss Gray is kind to animals, but I do not think so, for she keeps her pets prisoners—feeding them too much, and all for her own pleasure, until they become like spoilt children, peevish, and always wanting sweet things. Kind children love animals, and delight to see them free. In the Zoological Gardens animals are not pets; they have there plenty of room, and are nicely kept for our instruction. See, poor Jacko, the monkey, has grown too fat to leap, as in his native woods he used, from bough to bough. The poor gold fish have hardly room to turn in their glass prison: how they would enjoy a swim in the garden pond!

QUANDARY.—Poor Dame Partlet having got into the back yard cannot get out again. She is in a Quandary, for she fears the dogs will bite her—though their chains are not long enough. Keeper, the mastiff, is a noble fellow, and would not hurt women or children; neither would Nero, the bull-dog; he would rather face a lion or a wild ox: whilst Snap, the terrier, barks and snarls in the company of his brave companions.

Little boys and girls should not touch strange dogs, for they sometimes snap at those who are not familiar to them. To take food from dogs is not prudent, for they growl, bite, and are ill-tempered, like a little fellow would be if deprived of his dinner, after he had tasted the first morsel.

RIVALRY.—To compete for good is famous—such as little boys rivalling one another in a race up the Ladder of Learning—that is exercise of the mind. Here we have a picture of country boys exercising their strength—climbing up a pole covered with grease, for a prize of food for the body. The boy that wins the leg of mutton will be the hero of the fair, and be carried round the place on the shoulders of the men. See how they strive and tear to win the prize. I should not wonder if they all slipped down together, notwithstanding the encouraging cheers of the crowd. See how the man on the housetop swings his hat in the air, and the people applaud. A few inches higher, and the prize is won.

SLUGGARD.—Heavy-headed, sleepy Ned, awake, arise! You lazy fellow! Look at the clock! Eight hours' rest is enough for any little boy—and here you have taken nearly fourteen. All Sluggards should get their slates, and calculate how much time they waste every year—weeks that can never be regained. If you only lie in bed two hours later than you should every day, you lose more than one day in a week, or sixty-four days in the course of the year: which, at the end of seventy years, would be awful indeed! Twelve whole years lost! Lazy, idle people, never seem to have time for anything: industrious ones, time for anything and everything. I hope when little Ned sees his portrait he will be shocked with his appearance, and reform his ways.

[Pg 33] TOPSY-TURVY.—Well, of all the funny pictures in this droll book I think this the drollest—a big letter T resting on its top on the ceiling, like in an overturned doll's house, or a view taken by an artist standing upon his head. Turn it over, and see how comical it looks—everything appears to have lost its gravity.

Gravity means the power that holds us to the earth (as Papa's loadstone attracts the needle): if it were not for gravity, we could not move about. Some day you shall read in that nice book called the "Evenings at Home," about gravity, and why an apple falls to the ground. A great philosopher, Sir Isaac Newton, discovered why, as he lay under a tree. At a future time you will learn about gravity and many other things.

UNCOMMON VEGETATION. — Uncle Periwinkle was very kind; he loved nature and his nephews dearly. He wore green spectacles, a dressing-gown all covered with leaves, and a large straw hat; in fact he was very fond of gardening, and reared all kinds of odd plants — this his nephews knew, and determined to play a joke upon him — not a cruel, heartless joke, that would hurt or destroy anything: no! they were too kind for that. They only carefully tied the carpenter's planes upon the plane-tree, as if it were fruit — and some little boxes of all colours upon the box-tree, like blossom; so that when the old gentleman beheld it, he exclaimed — "Uncommon Vegetation!" upon which John and Walter came laughing out of the greenhouse to receive a bunch of fine grapes for their pleasant joke.

WONDER. — So, Master Ploughboy Giles, you are spending your penny and your holiday at the fair. You seem not a little astonished at what you have seen in that peep-show. Surely you cannot imagine that they are real; it is the magnifying power of the glasses that makes the pictures appear so large. The pyramids of Egypt are the largest stone buildings in the world, and the oldest; the Behemoth, a huge animal that existed thousands of years ago (but I do not think it had wings like a butterfly, as in the showman's picture); Daniel Lambert was an enormously fat man, who died a long time back. All these things must be in miniature if they are to be seen in that small box, very little larger than a dog's house.

XANTIPPE. — The comical event pictured here occurred more than two thousand years ago: Xantippe, the wife of the great and good philosopher Socrates, continually tormented him with her ill-humour — using him very cruelly — one day emptying a vessel of dirty water over her celebrated husband, whom she ought to have loved: he only remarked, that "after thunder there generally falls rain." Socrates lived in the refined city of Athens; he was one of the most eminent philosophers of Greece; he was very plain in person, as you perceive by the picture: but a man may be great and good, yet ugly, as Socrates was. The philosopher had enemies who sought his destruction; he was killed with poison. After his death his accusers were despised, as you will read in ancient history some day.

YEARN. — What have we here? Little Miss Cross vexed, just because she cannot get at the grapes. I am sure I should not like to have my portrait drawn with such a sullen face. She has been trying to take fruit without her aunt's permission, that very likely is unripe and improper for her. The walk in a delightful garden ought not to make her long to eat all the fruit she sets eyes upon, or wish to pick the sweet flowers, that last much longer upon the plants than when plucked. I perceive that the peevish young lady in the picture has been picking the flowers. See, they are strewn upon the seat beside her, under those dirty feet that have trodden down the beds of mould. I am afraid Miss Cross cannot be a joyous, happy child, because disobedient.

ZANY.—Finis is the Latin word for finish, and here it is the last droll picture—a Zany laughing at his portrait in this comical book, which he seems vastly to enjoy. What a droll fellow, to read with his head where his heels should be, like the clown in the pantomime. Look at his staff, the cock and bells, with which he dances, making a jingling noise. A Zany is not an idiot, but often a funny clever fellow, paid to make people laugh. We all like a good laugh sometimes. Many years ago kings used to keep jesters to amuse the company; King Henry the Eighth had a clever jester, called Will Somers, whose portrait was painted by a great artist named Holbein, which is now in the palace at Hampton Court, and may be seen by those who love pictures.

ILLUSTRATED

POPULAR

EDUCATIONAL WORKS,

PUBLISHED BY

WARD AND LOCK, 158, FLEET STREET,

LONDON.

Messrs. WARD and LOCK have much pleasure in announcing that they have just purchased the Copyrights of many of the Valuable Illustrated Educational Works lately published from the office of the *Illustrated London News*. The New Editions of these Popular

Books have been most carefully revised, and in their present state arrive as near perfection as possible. It is the intention of the present proprietors of these Educational Books to continue the Series, and they have already made arrangements to this effect.

The object of the Publishers is to supply a Series of Illustrated Volumes, adapted both for Schools and Private Study, which shall be accurate and complete text-books, *and at a price within the reach of every one.*

The old system of instruction, by which the names of things only were presented to the mind of the pupil, has been long admitted to have been imperfect and unsuccessful. With the young it is necessary to speak to the Eye, as well as to the Mind—to give a picture of an object as well as a description; and the adoption of such a plan of tuition is not only far more effective than that which is confined to words, but is at the same time much less irksome to the teacher, and more pleasant to the pupil. A greater interest is excited, and the representation of the object remains clear and distinct in the mind of the child long after the verbal description has passed away.

For Particulars of the "Illustrated Popular Educational Works," see Catalogue.

JUST READY,

THE ILLUSTRATED

WEBSTER

SPELLING BOOK.

Demy 8vo, embellished with upwards of

250 SPLENDID ENGRAVINGS

By Gilbert, Harvey, Dalziel, and other eminent artists. 128 pp., new and accented type, upon the principle of "Webster's Dictionary of the English Language." Cloth, gilt lettered, price 1s.; coloured, 2s.

. The "Illustrated Webster Spelling Book" has been most carefully compiled by an Eminent English Scholar, who is daily engaged in the tuition of youth, and, therefore, knows exactly what is really useful in a Spelling Book. The Reading Lessons are arranged upon a new progressive principle, exceedingly simple, and well adapted for the purpose. The Accented Type has been adopted, so as to ensure correct pronunciation. The old system of mis-spelling words is dangerous in the extreme, and, therefore, very justly, has now fallen into disuse. In a word, the "Illustrated Webster Spelling Book," whether considered in respect to its Typography, Binding, or Beauty of its Illustrations, must take the highest position as a School-Book, entirely setting aside the old-fashioned, and, in most instances, unintelligible—so called—helps to learning.

N.B.—Be careful to order "THE ILLUSTRATED WEBSTER SPELLING BOOK."

IN PREPARATION,

THE ILLUSTRATED

WEBSTER READER,

SERIES I.,

the illustrated webster reader, series ii.,

And other Educational Works.

JOHNSON AND WALKER SUPERSEDED.

Containing 10,000 more Words than Walker's Dictionary.

WEBSTER'S
POCKET PRONOUNCING DICTIONARY

Of the English Language;

Condensed from the Original Dictionary by Noah Webster, LL.D. With Accented Vocabularies of Classical, Scriptural, and Modern Geographical Names. Revised Edition, by William G. Webster (Son of Noah Webster). Royal 16mo, cloth gilt, 2s. 6d.; or strongly bound in roan, gilt, 3s.

. The Public will do well to be on their guard against unfair statements in reference to "Dr. Webster's" principle of pronunciation by accents. The old system of pronunciation by mis-spelling words has become obsolete, and Dr. Webster's method is universally acknowledged and adopted.

WEBSTER'S DICTIONARY
OF THE ENGLISH LANGUAGE
FOR THE MILLION!

Now Ready, Royal 16mo, bound in Cloth,
price eighteenpence,
WEBSTER'S DICTIONARY
OF THE ENGLISH LANGUAGE.

The extraordinary success attendant upon the publication of the Half-crown Edition of Webster's Pocket Pronouncing Dictionary of the English Language,—in the face of a most obstinate and inveterate opposition on the part of the proprietors of the out-of-date and worthless compilations, so called Dictionaries, printed from old stereotype plates, which have remained unaltered for years,—has induced Messrs. Ward and Lock to issue a CHEAPER EDITION FOR THE MILLION, price only **ONE SHILLING AND SIXPENCE!!!**

. The New Edition at **1s. 6d.** will, of course, be printed on thinner paper, but still the type will appear perfectly distinct. It is al-

most unnecessary to state, that only an enormous sale can reimbur-
se the Publishers in issuing an edition at so low a price as **1s. 6d.**;
still, Messrs. Ward and Lock feel assured that their good intentions
will be appreciated by an extensive and continually increasing sale.
"Webster" is now the only reliable authority on the English Language, and it is only right that every Englishman, however humble his
sphere, should be able to purchase the best English Dictionary.
Whilst the Cheaper Edition, at **1s. 6d.**, is well adapted for National
and British Schools, the Half-Crown Edition, on superior paper, and
bound in cloth, gilt lettered, will be always in demand for Schools of
a higher grade.

Third Edition, Revised.
THE ILLUSTRATED DRAWING BOOK.

Comprising a complete Introduction to Drawing and Perspective;
with Instructions for Etching on Copper or Steel, &c. &c. By Robert
Scott Burn. Illustrated with above 300 Subjects for Study in every
branch of Art. Demy 8vo, cloth, 2s.

*** This extremely popular and useful "Drawing Book" has been
thoroughly revised by the Author, and many new Illustrations are
added, thus rendering the **Third Edition** the most perfect Handbook of Drawing for Schools and Students.

*** "This is one of those cheap and useful publications lately issu-
ed by Ward and Lock. It is what it professes to be—an elementary
book, in which the rules laid down are simple and few, and the
drawings to be copied and studied are easily delineated and illust-
rative or first principles." — *Globe*.

*** "We could point to a work selling for twelve shillings not half
so complete, nor containing half the number of illustrations.
Perhaps of all the books for which the public are indebted to
Messrs. Ward and Lock this one will be found most extensively and

practically useful. It is the completest thing of the kind which has ever appeared." — *Tait's Magazine.*

. "This is a very capital Instruction Book, embodying a complete course of Lessons in Drawing, from the first Elements of Outline Sketching up to the most elaborate rules of the Art." — *Bristol Mercury.*

Just ready, Second Edition, Revised by the Author.
THE ILLUSTRATED ARCHITECTURAL, ENGINEERING,
AND MECHANICAL DRAWING BOOK.
By Robert Scott Burn. With 300 Engravings. Demy 8vo, cloth, 2s.

"This *Book* should be given to every youth, for amusement as well as for instruction." — *Taunton Journal.*

Third and Revised Edition.
MECHANICS AND MECHANISM.
By Robert Scott Burn. With about 250 Illustrations. Demy 8vo, cloth, 2s.

"One of the best-considered and most judiciously-illustrated elementary treatises on Mechanics and Mechanism which we have met with. The illustrations, diagrams, and explanations are skilfully introduced, and happily apposite — numerous and beautifully executed. As a handbook for the instruction of youth, it would be difficult to surpass it." — *Derby Mercury.*

Second Edition, Revised by the Author.
THE STEAM ENGINE:
ITS HISTORY AND MECHANISM.

Being Descriptions and Illustrations of the Stationary, Locomotive, and Marine Engine. By Robert Scott Burn. Demy 8vo, 200 pp., cloth, 3s.

. A most perfect compendium of everything appertaining to the Steam Engine. Mr. Burn treats his subjects in a thoroughly practical and popular manner, so that he who runs may read, and also understand.

"Mr. Burn's History of the Steam Engine treats an interesting subject in an admirably intelligible manner, and is illustrated by some excellent Diagrams. This is a book for the general reader, and deserves a wide circulation." — *Leader*.

Third Edition, Revised.
THE ILLUSTRATED PRACTICAL GEOMETRY.

Edited by Robert Scott Burn, Editor of the "Illustrated Drawing Book." Demy 8vo, cloth, 2s.

"Suited to the youthful mind, and calculated to assist Instructors, filled as it is with really good Diagrams and Drawings elucidatory of the text." — *Globe*.

LONDON: WARD AND LOCK, 158, FLEET STREET
AND ALL BOOKSELLERS.

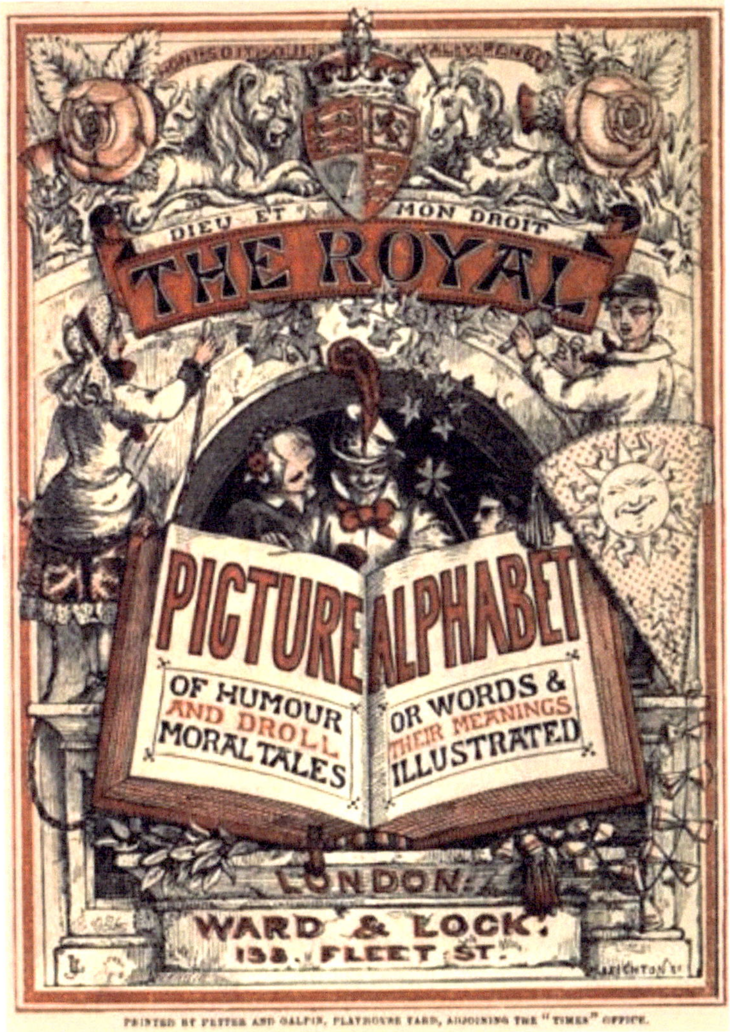